The Dragon
and the
Phoenix

A folktale from China

Retold by Lesley Sims
Illustrated by
Graham Philpot

Reading Consultant: Alison Kelly
Roehampton University

This is the story of

Dragon Mountain,

Phoenix Mountain

and a shining lake.

It begins thousands
of years ago, in China...

3

Long, long ago, a dragon lived beside a magic river.

A dark forest grew
on the other side of
the river.

Deep inside the forest
lived a phoenix.

Every day, the dragon
swam in the river.

8

Every day, the phoenix
flew in the sky above.

9

One day, they met on
an island in the river.

10

The dragon washed it
in the river.

The phoenix polished it
with a feather.

And the pebble became
a pearl.

The dragon and the
phoenix stayed on
the island...

...watching the pearl.

15

The pearl shone
brighter than stars...

...brighter than
the sun.

It was so bright, the
Queen of Heaven saw
it shine.

"I want that pearl!"
she said.

That night, she sent a
guard to steal it.

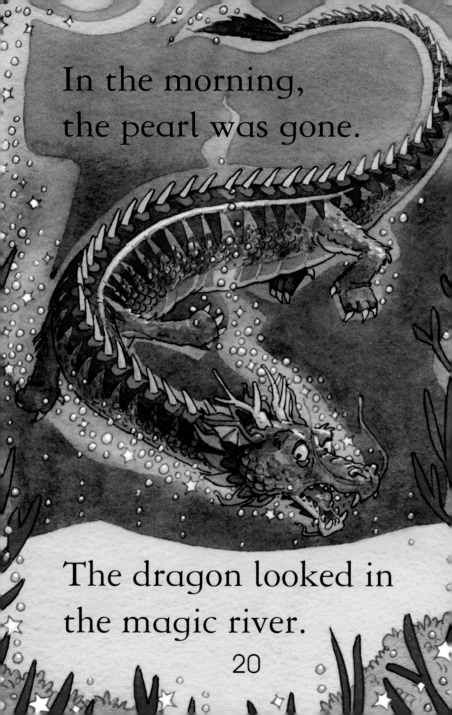

In the morning,
the pearl was gone.

The dragon looked in
the magic river.

The phoenix looked in
the dark forest.

No pearl there...

21

Then they saw it shining
in the sky.

They flew up to Heaven
and saw the Queen.

They are still there today.

PUZZLES

Puzzle 1

Put the pictures in order.

A

B

C

D

E

F

Puzzle 2

Can you spot the differences between the two pictures? There are six to find.

Puzzle 3
Find the opposites.

happy

summer

asleep

sad

winter

awake

Puzzle 4
Can you see...?

one pearl two fish

three flowers four pebbles

Answers to puzzles

Puzzle 1

B   F   A   C   E   D

Puzzle 2

Puzzle 3

happy

sad

asleep

awake

winter

summer

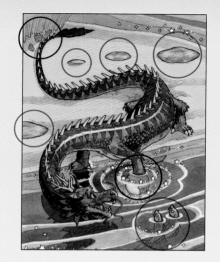

The Dragon and the Phoenix

This story is based on *The Bright Pearl,* a folktale from China. In Chinese stories, dragons and phoenixes are often shown together. Chinese dragons have lots of magical powers and can even fly without wings.

Designed by
Catherine-Anne MacKinnon

First published in 2007 by Usborne Publishing Ltd., Usborne House,
83-85 Saffron Hill, London EC1N 8RT, England. www.usborne.com
Copyright © 2007 Usborne Publishing Ltd.

32